104918

# Dear Tooth Fairy

## A Harry & Emily Adventure

### Karen Gray Ruelle

Holiday House / New York

Reading level: 2.4

Text and illustrations copyright © 2006 by Karen Gray Ruelle
All Rights Reserved
Printed in the United States of America
www.holidayhouse.com
First Edition
1 3 5 7 9 10 8 6 4 2

Library of Congress Cataloging-in-Publication Data
Ruelle, Karen Gray.
Dear Tooth Fairy / Karen Gray Ruelle.—1st ed.
p. cm. — (A Harry & Emily adventure)
Summary: When her tooth becomes loose, Emily excitedly writes
to the Tooth Fairy and tries to help the tooth fall out.
ISBN-10: 0-8234-1929-0 (hardcover)
ISBN-10: 0-8234-1984-3 (pbk.)
ISBN-13: 978-0-8234-1929-6 (hardcover)
ISBN-13: 978-0-8234-1984-5 (pbk.)
[1. Teeth—Fiction. 2. Tooth fairy—Fiction.] I. Title.
PZ7.R88525Dea 2006
[E]—dc22
2005046368

# Contents

# 1. Emily's Big News

Emily's tooth did not feel right.

It was a bottom tooth.

It was on the right side.

When she touched her tooth,
it jiggled.

She ran to tell her big brother, Harry.

"Look!" she said.

She opened her mouth wide.

"I don't see anything," said Harry.

Emily jiggled her tooth.

"You have a loose tooth," said Harry.

"It's my FIRST loose tooth!" said Emily.

"Let's tell Mom and Dad," said Harry.

They ran downstairs
to tell Emily's news.
"What happens when my tooth
falls out?" asked Emily.
"The Tooth Fairy comes
while you are asleep," said Harry.

"When you go to bed,
  put the tooth under your pillow.
  The Tooth Fairy will take it.
  She will leave a treasure in its place."
"I can't wait to see her!
  She must be very pretty!" said Emily.
"You can't see her," said Harry.
"You will be asleep when she comes."
"We'll see," said Emily.

# 2. A Very Loose Tooth

Emily wanted the Tooth Fairy
to know about her loose tooth.
So she wrote her a letter.
She wrote down her address.

Dear Tooth Fairy,

My tooth is loose.

Get ready!

From your friend Emily

P.S. I like all kinds of treasures.

She wanted the Tooth Fairy
to find the right house.
She drew a picture of herself.
Now the Tooth Fairy would know
what she looked like.
Emily wrote to
the Tooth Fairy every day.
The next day she wrote,

Dear Tooth Fairy,

My tooth will fall out soon.

I like bracelets and rings.

From your friend Emily

P.S. Pink and green are my

favorite colors.

The next day she wrote,

Dear Tooth Fairy,

My tooth is nearly out.

I like magic wands and fairy wings.

From your friend Emily

P.S. I also like unicorns.

Every day, Emily's tooth
got looser and looser.
She helped by jiggling it
whenever she could.
Finally Emily knew her tooth
was ready to fall out.

She wrote to the Tooth Fairy,

Dear Tooth Fairy,

Tonight is the night!

My tooth will fall out today.

I hope you are ready

with my treasure!

From your friend Emily

P.S. How will I know it is you?

What do you look like?

Emily waited all day
for her tooth to fall out.
She wiggled it.
She jiggled it.
The tooth would not come out.
"What will I do if the Tooth Fairy
comes tonight?" she asked Harry.
"I hope the Tooth Fairy
does not get mad."

# 3. Apples, Peanut Butter, and Cookies

Emily had to get her tooth out.

Harry said, "Why don't you

eat an apple?"

"Yuck," said Emily.

She did not like apples.

But she did not want that tooth

to stay in.

She bit into three apples.

But her tooth moved

out of the way each time.

"Try some peanut butter," said Harry.
Emily ate a peanut-butter-and-
honey sandwich.
It was yummy.

But it did not help one bit.

"Maybe cookies would help,"

said Emily.

She ate four.

But that tooth would not come out.

Before bed, Harry and Emily's
mother read them a story.
Emily jiggled her tooth
the whole time.

Then Harry and Emily had hot chocolate.

Emily bit into the marshmallow.

*POP!*

It pulled her tooth right out!

"Hooray for marshmallows!" said Emily.

Their father put Emily's tooth
in a little treasure box.

Emily put the box under her pillow.

Then she brushed
her other teeth.

Then she got into bed.

# 4. The Tooth Fairy

Emily reached under her pillow.

She checked on her tooth.

She closed her eyes.

She counted sheep.

She counted bunnies.

She even counted frogs.

But she just could not sleep.

Then she heard tapping.

Maybe the Tooth Fairy

was tapping on the window!

Emily ran over to see.

But there was no Tooth Fairy.

The pouring rain was tapping.

"Oh no," said Emily.

"What if it is too rainy

for the Tooth Fairy?

What if she does not come?"

Emily woke up Harry.

"What is the matter?" he asked.

"It's raining," said Emily.

"What if the Tooth Fairy doesn't
want to come out in the rain?"

"Don't worry," said Harry.

"She probably has
an umbrella."

Just then there was a loud
clap of thunder.

"Oh no!" said Emily.

"What if the Tooth Fairy
is afraid of thunder?
She might not come."

"The Tooth Fairy will come,"
said Harry.

"But you have to be asleep.
She will not come
if you are awake."

Emily went back to her room.
She got into bed.
She snuggled way down
under her blanket.
She tried as hard as she could
to fall asleep.

# 5. Perfect Treasures

The next morning when Emily
woke up, the sun was shining.
She remembered about her tooth.
She reached under her pillow.
The treasure box was still there.
There was also a note.
It said *EMILY* on it.
She opened it up and read it.

Dear Emily,

Thank you for the tooth.

I hope you like your treasures.

Here is my picture.

From the Tooth Fairy

There was a pretty picture of
the Tooth Fairy, just for Emily.
The Tooth Fairy had green fairy wings.
She had a magic wand.

Emily opened the treasure box.

Her tooth was gone.

In its place were a ring
and a bracelet.

They were pink and green.

They had unicorns on them.

They were perfect!

Emily put on her ring and bracelet.

She went to show Harry.

"Now I know what the Tooth Fairy
looks like," said Emily.

"She is very pretty."

"How do you know?" asked Harry.

"She gave me an extra-special
  treasure," said Emily.
  And Emily showed Harry her picture.
"Next time the Tooth Fairy comes,
  I will stay awake," said Emily.
"I want to thank her for my treasures."

"You will have to wait for another
loose tooth," said Harry.
"I'm sure I will have one soon,"
said Emily.
And she went to get the marshmallows,
just in case.